OUT OF THIS WORLD

Published by Curious Fox, an imprint of Capstone Global Library Limited, 264 Banbury Road, Oxford, OX2 7DY – Registered company number: 6695582

www.curious-fox.com

Text © 2017 Raymond Bean
Illustrations © 2017 Stone Arch Books

The author's moral rights are hereby asserted.

Illustrations by Matthew Vimislik

ISBN 978 1 78202 565 8
20 19 18 17 16
10 9 8 7 6 5 4 3 2 1

A CIP catalogue for this book is available from the British Library.

Printed and bound in China

OUT OF THIS WORLD

THE CURSE
OF MARS

by Raymond Bean

Curious Fox
a capstone company-publishers for children

CONTENTS

INTRODUCTION

My name is Starr. I'm just like every other ten-year-old girl I know, with one big difference: I live in space.

You see, my mum is a world-class astronaut, scientist and all-round super-genius. She was chosen to be the first person to move her entire family to space. Now she's not just my mum, she's also in charge of the world's most advanced space station.

Dad is a documentary filmmaker. He's making a movie about our family being the first family to ever live in space. It's not like we're actors or anything. He just films us doing our everyday stuff like eating, playing and brushing our teeth.

I have a thirteen-year-old brother called Apollo. He thinks he's cooler than winter.

Cosmo is my super-cute, five-year-old brother.

If you ask me, he *is* cooler than winter. We call him "Cozzie" for short.

We're helping to lead the new world of space tourism so that people can take holidays in space. I like to call them space holidays.

The head of the entire space programme is Mrs Sosa. She's my mum's boss. Her granddaughter, Tia, and I work together. Tia trains kids on Earth to get them ready for space. I help them with life in space once they're on the station.

My best friend, Allison, thinks I'll forget all about her now that I live in space, but just because I live in space doesn't mean I don't need my best friend.

I may be an ordinary girl, but my life is completely out of this world!

Chapter 1

PANIC AND FEAR

I was in my pod, looking out into space and trying to get a better look at Mars. My phone buzzed and I tapped the screen to answer. I grabbed hold of a stabilizer bar to keep my balance. Floating in zero gravity can be tricky!

"Hey, Allison," I said. Allison and I talk all the time, even though she's on Earth, and I was in our space station approaching Mars. Normally, it would take about six minutes for the phone signal to reach Earth from where we were, but Professor Will invented an amazing new phone system so we can make calls just as we would on Earth. Professor Will is great — his job is to build whatever machines we might need to help us with our missions in space.

"Hey! Are you there yet?" she asked.

"Not yet, and it feels like we've been travelling forever," I said. I wasn't exaggerating either. We'd been travelling for weeks on our way to visit and explore Mars.

"When do you think you'll get there?" Allison asked.

"Mum said we'll get there today, but I'll believe it when I see it."

Cozzie, my little brother, zipped into my room on his cruiser. "Starr! Did you see it?"

"Hey, Cozzie!" Allison called.

Cozzie put his face up super-close to the screen and said, "Hi, Allison! I wish you could see it too!" He pointed outside my pod.

"Deimos!" I shouted. "Finally! We're here!"

"What?" Allison asked.

"Outside the pod," I said. I turned my phone around so she could see. "It's Deimos, one of Mars's moons. It has two moons: Deimos and Phobos."

"That's so weird!" she exclaimed.

My phone buzzed. I had another call coming in. "Tia's calling," I said to Allison.

"I'll let you go. Have fun and keep in touch!" she said as she waved goodbye.

"Bye!" Cozzie and I shouted.

I hung up. "Hey, Tia," I said, answering her call.

"According to my calculations, you should be able to see Deimos," she said.

"I'm fine, Tia. How are you?" I asked sarcastically. Sometimes Tia can be a little abrupt.

"What? Oh, sorry . . . How are you?" she asked when she realized I was being sarcastic.

"Fine, thanks for asking," I said, winking at Cozzie.

Tia's grandmother, Mrs Sosa, leaned into view. "Hi, kids! How's the view of Deimos?"

"It looks like a giant, floating tooth," I said excitedly. It had craters on its surface like Earth's moon, but it was much smaller. Deimos was greyish, with a bit of a red tint.

Cozzie giggled. "It does look like a tooth! I think it has a few cavities too."

My older brother, Apollo, cruised in. Our cruisers help us move around the space station faster. They're like small jets that we hold on to and steer. They're so much fun! Apollo clicked his cruiser off and attached it to the pack on his back. "Pretty sweet!" he announced, pointing outside at Deimos. "But did you know Deimos's name means 'panic'?" Apollo added ominously.

"Really?" Cozzie asked, fear crossing his face.

I glared at Apollo and shook my head. He's always trying to scare Cozzie, and it drives me crazy!

"It's named after a Greek god," Tia announced.

"Does it mean I should panic?" Cozzie asked hesitantly.

"Well, Mars has another moon that's even bigger named Phobos. Its name means 'fear,'" Apollo added, "so probably."

"You aren't even going to the moons," Tia reminded Cozzie.

"True, but if the moons are named for panic and fear, imagine how scary Mars must be," Apollo said, eyeing Cozzie. "It might even be cursed."

"Ignore him," I told Cozzie.

"The names of the moons are Panic and Fear!" Cozzie shouted, terror in his eyes. He clicked on his cruiser and raced from my room. I heard his calls for my mother trailing off through the space station. "Mars is cursed!" he shouted.

Chapter 2

MARTIAN SELFIE

Apollo smiled mischievously as we cruised out of my room. "I was only trying to teach him about Mars's moons," he said. We cruised next to each other so we could still talk.

"Right," I said, feeling as if we were about to get into an argument. "You shouldn't scare him like that," I said. "Also, did you know Mrs Sosa was listening in on the call?"

"She was?" Apollo asked, looking embarrassed. Mrs Sosa was in charge of the entire space programme. If

Mum knew how Apollo was behaving in front of Mrs Sosa, she'd be really angry, and Apollo knew it. "I'll find Cozzie and tell him I was only messing around," he said.

We cruised into the control pod, where Mum and the crew steer the station. It was crowded, and it seemed as if everyone on the ship was already gathered there to see Mars. Mum was seated in the captain's chair. She looked annoyed. Cozzie was on her lap and looked as if he'd been crying.

"I'm *SO* sorry!" Apollo pleaded before Mum could say anything. We shut down our cruisers and floated in the room with the rest of the crew.

"This is a big moment, Apollo," Mum reminded him, pointing to Mars. "Space can be scary enough. You shouldn't make it worse for him."

"Cozzie, I was just messing around. There's nothing to be afraid of," Apollo said, glancing at Mum for her reaction. She turned her attention back to Mars. Apollo looked like he wasn't sure if he was off the hook.

Dad, who'd been videoing Mars, pointed his camera away from Mars and turned it towards us in an attempt to change the subject. "There it is, kids. We're the first people to ever visit Mars! What do you think?"

I'd seen lots of photos and videos of Mars, but seeing it with my own two eyes was really spectacular. We were close enough now that I could make out canyons and even large boulders on the surface. It was red, as I had expected. It was empty-looking, as I had expected. Dad was looking for me to say something interesting to the camera, so I said, "It's beautiful."

"What is beautiful about it?" he asked.

"It's just so still. It reminds me of a huge, red desert."

"It really is pretty," Mum said, no longer mad at Apollo and refocused on Mars. "Talk about a dream come true! If you had told me ten years ago that I'd be orbiting Mars with my family, I would have never believed it."

"It looks creepy," Cozzie said, snuggling closer to Mum.

We all looked at Apollo. He pretended not to notice and looked out on Mars. "I'm with Starr. I think it looks beautiful," he said. I didn't buy his nice-guy routine.

Mum turned her attention to the group. I took a closer look around too. Two of my favourite crew members, Kathy and Professor Will, were there. They both waved to me, and I waved back. We had a lot of scientists and their families on board and they all seemed to be there too. I guess everyone wanted to be there for the historic event. We were the first group of people to reach Mars . . . EVER!

"Welcome to Mars!" Mum announced. The group clapped and someone let out a high-pitched whistle. Dad panned the group with his camera. I could tell he didn't want to miss a second of everyone's reaction to seeing Mars for the first time. Cozzie finally smiled.

"You're the first humans to visit the red planet in history," Mum continued. "Congratulations! Please enjoy the rest of your day as the station orbits the red planet and the crew and I prepare to land. Take lots of photos and videos. The world is eager to see what we're seeing! History will want to see what we are seeing!"

The crowd cheered again. People shook hands and hugged.

I looked around for my team. On every trip, I'm in charge of a few kids. On this trip I was in charge of a boy named Raj and a girl named Yuna.

Raj came from India and was really smart. During the journey to Mars, he'd taken apart just about every electronic device he could get his hands on and put it back together again. He reminded me of a young Professor Will.

Yuna was from Japan. Whenever we had any free time, she painted. I'd never seen anyone paint in space until I met her. She brought lots of art supplies on the trip and was having a hard time keeping track of them. In the microgravity of space, anything that's not secured or placed in a bag floats away. I'd found a few of her pencils and a tube of paint floating around the station.

When I spotted Raj and Yuna, they were taking pictures. I floated over and joined them.

Working with Raj and Yuna had been a challenge for me because English was their second language. They could speak English a little, but when we tried talking, someone always ended up getting confused. Since our phones translated our texts into our first language, it was easier to communicate by texting.

I texted: *Welcome to Mars!*

Their phones buzzed. They read the texts and gave a thumbs-up. Raj waved for Yuna and me to come closer. He took a picture of all three of us with his phone. Then he texted it to us. My phone buzzed. It said: *FIRST MARTIAN SELFIE EVER!*

We all smiled. I forwarded it to Allison and Tia.

Early in the trip, Mum had told me that working with Raj and Yuna was actually one of the experiments the crew had designed for the trip to Mars. They wanted to study how kids would work together in space if they speak different languages. Adults had already had to deal with language differences on the International Space Station, but it was the first time for kids.

I was a little frustrated because the kids who Apollo was working with all spoke English. It made his job ten times easier than mine. Mum said I should take it as a compliment that the crew trusted me with such an important experiment. I tried to think of it that way, but it still didn't seem fair.

Chapter 3

MARTIAN MASTER

Later in the day, there was a sense of excitement on the ship like never before. People zipped in every direction preparing for the landing on Mars. Raj and Yuna stayed with their families, taking pictures and getting ready for the landing. Both of their parents were scientists and would be very busy while on Mars. While their parents were working, it would be up to me to keep Raj and Yuna safe and entertained. No pressure!

I took off on my cruiser. I wanted to take a look at some of the other experiments the crew would be doing once on the surface. Crew members were preparing to measure wind, look for water, take air and soil temperatures, and all kinds of other cool experiments.

I found Kathy busy at work. Kathy raises fish and plants together in an amazing interconnected system called aquaponics. Most of the vegetables, fruits, and fish we eat on the station come from her work. I'm her number-one helper.

Kathy was moving tomato plants from small planters to larger containers. "Hi, Starr, are you ready for the landing?" she asked.

"I can't wait," I said. "What are you going to do with all these plants?"

"I want to see if we can grow plants on Mars. I hope to build permanent greenhouses on the surface. If we can learn to grow crops there, people might be able to live on Mars permanently in the future."

"But how will the plants get water?" I asked.

"The pod will be completely sealed from the outside

environment. Any water that is placed inside the pod will stay inside it. If I get it right, it should create a complete water cycle."

"But Mars is freezing cold," I reminded her.

"True, but the Sun shines on Mars about the same number of hours per day as it does on Earth. The pod will capture the sunlight and use it to heat up the pod. Since Mars is further from the Sun, the sunlight isn't as strong as on Earth. The pod is designed to magnify the heat from the Sun, creating a very warm and humid environment for the plants."

"That's cool!"

"I'm having fun with it," she said. Kathy looked up at me curiously. "How are things going with your team? You might have the most difficult experiment of the mission."

I was happy that Kathy understood that working with Raj and Yuna wasn't easy.

"They're really nice kids, but it's been quite hard," I said. "As you know, we can't talk to each other easily."

"I'm sure you'll find a solution," she said, getting back to work.

"I hope so," I said. "I'm going to take off and see what Professor Will is up to. Maybe I'll talk to him about it."

When I cruised into Professor Will's pod, he was tightening something on a vehicle I'd never seen before.

"Hi, Starr!" he said. "Are you as excited as I am to become a Martian?"

I smiled. "You bet."

"What do you think of my latest invention?"

"It looks amazing," I said. "What is it?" It looked like an aeroplane, a spaceship, and a rover all mixed together. The outside was dark green with black-tinted windows.

"I call it the Martian Master, or MM for short!"

"Cool!"

It reminded me of one of Cozzie's toys that changed from a robot to a truck.

"The MM can move several different ways," Professor Will said. "If the weather is calm, it can fly above the surface, much like an aeroplane. But sometimes Mars is very windy and has sand storms. When this happens, the vehicle can simply roll along the surface like a rover. For long distances, it functions like a rocket ship and can travel at very high speeds. It may be my best invention."

The door opened on the driver's side and Cozzie stuck his head out. "It's AWESOME!" he exclaimed.

"I didn't know you were in there!" I said.

"I'm helping Professor Will build it!"

"Oh wow," I said, smiling. I turned to the professor. "Can I climb inside with him?"

"Of course," he said. I climbed in on the passenger side. The cockpit was larger than I expected. It had two rows of seats and could easily hold six people.

"It's green," Cozzie said. "Do you know why that's important?" he asked seriously.

I thought about it for a moment. "No, why?"

"Because everything else on Mars is red, so the green makes it stand out. Professor Will told me."

"That makes sense," I said. "Was painting it green your idea?"

"No, I would have painted it all different colours . . . with zigzags . . . and stars," Cozzie said.

"Your team will have access to your very own Martian Master," I heard Professor Will say from outside the MM. "I built eight of them altogether."

"Can the kids fly it?" I asked hopefully.

"Sure, with some training. I've made it very user-friendly. The Martian Master can even fly itself if needed. All you have to do is tell it where you want to go and it will do the rest."

"I can't wait to give it a try."

Chapter 4

NO MORE TEXTING

Landing on Mars the next day was out of this world! Raj, Yuna, Cozzie, and I sat buckled into our seats in the control pod as Mum steered the massive station towards the surface.

The station is made up of clear, round pods. Each one is connected to the others by clear tubes. The pods can be arranged in lots of different ways to change the outside shape of the station. They had been arranged in the shape of a spaceship for our long trip to Mars, but now they changed position as we lowered to the surface.

"What's it doing?" I asked Mum.

"The pods were packed tightly together during our trip here," she said. "I'm shifting them around so they will spread out across the Martian surface. Each pod will anchor into place and help keep the station secure."

The station slowly lowered until it made contact with the Martian surface. By spreading out the pods, the station covered a much larger area.

We gazed out on the view and no one said anything. I could hardly believe my eyes. We were really on Mars. But I couldn't help thinking it was a little creepy. In every direction rocks, red dust, and hills stretched as far as I could see. We were all alone and very far from home. I remembered what Apollo said about panic and fear, and got an uneasy feeling.

Mum broke the silence. "When you unbuckle, remember that there is gravity on Mars. Don't expect to float around anymore. You'll be walking again, and it's been a while, so be careful as you get your legs used to it."

She unbuckled and got up slowly.

I did the same. I felt pretty unstable. My legs were sort of wobbly. I had to hold on to my chair for a few seconds to get used to standing again. The bottom of our pod had flattened out to become a floor. "Look at the bottom of the pod," I said.

"The lower part of each pod flattens out when we land to give us a floor to walk on," Mum said. "Otherwise we'd have to walk on curved surfaces throughout the station."

Tia texted. She must have been watching the live stream back at the training centre: *Congratulations!*

I felt a bit bad for Tia. I knew she would do anything to be with us on Mars. I snapped a few pictures and sent them to her and Allison in a group text. I was a little worried they'd only make Tia jealous, but I wanted to include them. I wrote: *Getting used to walking again.*

Then I group-texted Raj and Yuna: *What do you think?*

They texted right back.

Yuna wrote: *Amazing!*

Then Raj wrote: *Can't wait to check it out!*

My phone buzzed again. It was Allison: *I can't believe you're on Mars!*

I looked up and noticed Mum staring at me. "What?" I asked.

"We've just landed on Mars, and you've hardly looked up from your phone."

"It's the only way I can communicate with Raj and Yuna," I said.

"I realize that, but constantly looking at your phones is very distracting for you."

"I know, but it's the only way. We need some other kind of technology. Something that can translate what each of us says without having to look at our phones all the time."

"You're smart kids. You'll figure something out."

I looked at Mum and then at Raj and Yuna. "I think I might have an idea."

"I knew you would," Mum said.

I texted Raj and Yuna: *Follow me.*

We walked off towards Professor Will's pod. It was so strange to walk again. We all kept giggling. We didn't have to say anything. We were experiencing the same thing, and we all found it funny. I knew we needed a better way to have that connection without using our phones.

When we got there, Professor Will was under a Martian Master. He popped his head out when he heard us.

"Hello, Starr!" he said.

"Hey, Professor. I know you're really busy, but I wondered if you might be able to help us with something."

"Of course! What do you have in mind?"

"We've been texting each other the whole trip, and that's sort of worked up until now," I said. "But I think we're going to have a hard time once we're on Mars. Also, Mum is concerned that we're always looking at our phones."

"What do you have in mind?"

I texted Raj and Yuna: *The professor is going to help*

us communicate better. *I'm getting tired of texting, how about you?*

They both texted back that they were tired of it too.

Raj added: *We need some kind of audio translator. Texting is slow and distracting. I've had several ideas too. Does the professor have a supply room?*

I texted Raj to say I was thinking the same thing. Then I explained what we had in mind to Professor Will and asked him if we could tinker around in his supply room. The professor scratched his head a few times and then said, "Right this way."

The supply room was bigger than I expected. There were lots of containers holding all kinds of electronic equipment. Raj looked like he was in heaven.

Yuna texted: *We need a device that translates what we say, not only what we type.*

Raj nodded and typed: *It needs to have a voice feature too so we don't have to keep looking at our phones.*

I typed: *What if we put it in our space suit helmets?*

"They're in my workshop," the professor said, looking over my shoulder at my phone. "I'll get them for you."

Raj immediately started taking his phone apart. I grabbed a container full of wires. Yuna took out a notebook from her backpack and started drawing a design. I had a feeling we were on to something big.

Chapter 5

FINAL TEST

Later that day, Apollo, Cozzie, and I were going through a last-minute Martian space suit check with Mum and Dad. We were in a special training pod that created the conditions we would experience when out on the Martian surface the next day. It was the last time we'd practise before experiencing the real thing.

"Tomorrow, when we explore the surface, you'll collect rock samples," Mum said. "For larger samples, you'll have bags to put the rocks in, and you can place smaller samples in the pockets of your suit. As you know, there used to be water on Mars. One of our goals for the mission is to find more evidence of water on the surface of Mars. The more samples we collect, the better the chances are that we'll discover something amazing."

"Where did all the water go?" Cozzie asked.

"What do you think?" Dad asked me. He was filming.

"Maybe someone drank it all," Cozzie said.

Dad smiled.

"But no one lives on Mars," I said, smiling at Cozzie.

"What about Martians?" he asked. "I bet they're thirsty."

"We are the only Martians," Mum said.

"That we know of," Apollo added. It was as if he couldn't help himself from trying to frighten Cozzie.

We all glared at Apollo. He smirked and said, "Sorry."

If you were sorry, you would stop, I thought.

"In a few moments the pod is going to open slightly, which will allow the Martian atmosphere in," Mum said. "The temperature will drop, but we should stay comfortable and safe. Are you ready?"

"I hope my cameras hold up," Dad said.

My heart pounded in my chest. I knew we were safe, but it was still a little scary. What if Mars really did have some sort of curse?

"Here it comes," Mum said, pressing a button on the side of the pod. Vents in the side of the pod opened, letting in the Martian atmosphere. The computer screen on the wall displayed the temperature. It dropped to seventy-three degrees below zero Celsius. The computer displayed that there was almost no oxygen and mostly carbon dioxide. Thankfully the suit continued to provide us with oxygen to breathe.

"What's the big deal?" Cozzie asked. "I don't feel any different."

"That's the idea," Dad said.

"Perfect!" Mum said, smiling. "The space suits are absolutely perfect."

It was hard to imagine that the temperature was so cold and there was really no oxygen outside, because I felt perfectly normal. We stayed in the suits and the simulator for about thirty more minutes as we ran tests on the suits. Mum had us run in place, jump around, and even fall a few times.

When she was convinced that the suits could handle Mars, Mum pressed the button again. The vents closed back up.

"We can take our helmets off in a few seconds," Mum said. "The pod is filling back up with oxygen and heating the air so we can breathe safely and be comfortable."

I looked at the monitor on the side of the pod measuring the oxygen levels and the temperature. The numbers were going up really fast until they stopped and a buzzer sounded. Mum took off her helmet and told us we could do the same.

"Well," Mum said. "That's the last test. We're all set to make our first Martian walk tomorrow."

My phone buzzed. It was Professor Will.

"Hi, Starr," he said. "Can you come to my pod? I think we have something you're going to like. I'll need your helmet."

"I'll be there in a few minutes," I said excitedly.

Raj and Yuna had kept working with the professor while I was at the safety check with my family. When I got there, Raj and Yuna had on their space helmets. Professor Will looked as proud as a peacock. I was really excited to see how our design had turned out.

Raj waved for me to hand him my helmet. I handed it to him, and he pulled out the liner and installed lots of wires and a small speaker. He also put in what looked like a small computer chip and screwed it all in place. Then he placed the liner carefully back.

"That looks amazing," I said.

He handed me my helmet and I put it on.

"Okay," the professor said. "Say something."

"What should I say?" I asked.

Raj and Yuna giggled. "Can they understand me?" I asked. "Can you understand me?!" I asked.

They giggled louder. Yuna said something in Japanese, but in my helmet I heard a computer voice say, "Starr, I can understand you can!" It wasn't perfect, but I got the idea of what she was saying.

"Raj, can you understand me too?" I asked.

He said something in Hindi, but I heard the computer voice say, "Yes, please and thank you!"

"It's still a bit glitchy, but it's better than texting," Professor Will said. "You'll have to be careful not to jar your helmets too much. The wiring is very delicate. You don't want to damage the speaker. You'll really need to use that on Mars. I'll keep working on it."

We all nodded that we understood, but couldn't stop talking and laughing. We could finally understand each other . . . sort of.

Chapter 6

HOLD ON TIGHT

The next morning, I was super-excited. We were going to take our first Martian walk! I didn't know whether I was more excited about the Martian walk or the ability to talk with Raj and Yuna without having to text them.

After breakfast, everyone met in the exit pod and put on their space suits.

A green light inside the exit pod blinked a few times, and Mum announced that it was time for us to go outside. A door slid open, and suddenly there was nothing between Mars's surface and us. Mum went out first and then the rest of us followed.

"Everyone is free to have fun and explore, but the plan is to collect as many samples as we can," said Mum. "If you see any rocks or other deposits that you think look interesting, please place them in your bag or in your pockets. For all we know, one of you might discover a Martian fossil or a deposit containing water. Kids, Professor Will updated the translation feature in your helmets. I think you'll find it more accurate now."

"I can't believe this!" Yuna said, walking away from the pod.

"I know," I said. "To move faster, try skipping."

"Wait up," Raj called, waving goodbye to his parents.

We all skipped off in the same direction. The ground reminded me a lot of the desert. I immediately noticed a small pile of rocks that looked interesting. I took out my bag and stopped. Raj and Yuna stopped there too. "Let's take some samples," I said.

"Wow! I love collecting rocks and shells on the beach at home," Yuna said.

"But this is way more exciting," Raj added.

"Maybe your mum will let me paint some of the Martian rocks when we get back in the station," Yuna said.

Dad bounced up to us. He looked funny bouncing across the surface like a bunny. He was recording us on his camera, which made him look even sillier. We waved, and he recorded us collecting samples and bouncing around the surface.

I spotted Apollo and the kids from his team in the distance. They were kicking something back and forth. "What is that?" I asked Dad.

"It's a soccer ball."

"Football!" Raj declared. "Football on Mars!"

I quickly realized that when I said "soccer" and he said "football," we were talking about the same thing.

"Can we play?" Raj asked.

"Sure," Dad said. "Skip on over and join in. It's the first-ever sporting event on Mars! The work can wait for a while."

Kicking a ball on Mars is much different than doing the same thing on Earth. Since gravity isn't as strong on Mars, the ball travelled much further when we kicked it. It was going so far that if we were on Earth, it would have looked as if we were professionals.

Apollo had just launched a kick way into the atmosphere above us. When we looked up to see it, we spotted Professor Will soaring above us in the Martian Master. The ball sailed up on a collision course with the MM. Professor Will tried to move out of the way, but the ball smacked into the MM anyway.

Everyone cringed. "I didn't mean it," Apollo said sheepishly.

The MM wobbled a bit, turned, and headed back towards the station.

"Let's go see if he's all right!" Dad shouted.

Professor Will had just landed when we reached him.

"I'm so sorry!" Apollo pleaded when the professor got out.

"That was some shot!" he exclaimed. "You really gave me a scare." The professor crawled underneath the MM to take a look.

"Thanks," Apollo said proudly.

"Is there any damage?" I asked.

"The MM is designed to handle far worse things than getting hit with a ball, but I'll double-check everything anyway."

After a quick safety check, we all watched as Professor Will demonstrated the Martian Master. First, he hovered above us. Then, he blasted off like a spaceship and zoomed out of sight. In no time at all, he was back and landed on the surface. He rolled over to where we stood and stopped. We were all speechless, even Mum.

He got out and said, "The Martian Master works even better than I'd imagined. Cozzie, great work!"

Cozzie gave a thumbs-up and said, "No problem."

I could see why the professor painted the Martian Master green. It made it stand out against the red surface.

"I'd like to give everyone a chance to explore with an MM. Inside you'll see a touch screen with a map of the entire planet. The map can use your location to guide you anywhere on Mars. I've designed them so children can use them as well as the adults. If for any reason you lose control while operating the vehicle, the computers will take over. If you see Apollo playing soccer, avoid him at all cost," he joked. There were several giggles.

"In order to be extra-safe, though," Mum said, "we'll have an adult go in each Martian Master."

Dad went with Apollo and his team, and Mum and Cozzie went with my group and me.

"Can I drive?" Cozzie asked, climbing in.

"Let Starr start off," Mum answered. "After she gets the hang of it, maybe you can sit on Mummy's lap and have a turn." Cozzie didn't seem thrilled, but he agreed.

Cozzie climbed in the back with Mum, and I climbed

in the front with Raj and Yuna. I touched the control-panel screen and the Martian Master turned on.

It displayed a map of the area around us and highlighted some of the interesting things that we might want to see.

"Olympus Mons!" Raj exclaimed. "We have to see Olympus Mons!"

"That's fine with me," Yuna added.

I knew from my research that Olympus Mons was the highest point on Mars. "It's the tallest volcano in the solar system," I said.

"Volcano!" Cozzie exclaimed. "We'll get burned by the lava!"

"It's not active," Yuna said.

"It's perfectly safe," Mum assured him.

Raj turned back to look at Cozzie. "Would you like to press the screen and tell the Martian Master where we're going, Cozzie?" he asked.

Cozzie lit up. He looked at Mum, and she nodded that it was fine. He unbuckled quickly and leaned over the seat. "Hold on tight!" he shouted, pressing the screen.

Chapter 7

OLYMPUS MONS

The other Martian Masters lifted off the surface before us and headed out in different directions. I started our liftoff procedure and we slowly lifted off the ground.

Red dust kicked up, and then we were high enough above the surface that the dust cleared and we had a sweeping view of the Martian terrain. Yuna pointed to the screen. A small icon showed our ship's location. There were several other icons headed off in different directions to show where the other ships were going. We seemed to be the only ones heading to Olympus Mons.

"Olympus Mons is three times higher than Mount Everest on Earth," Mum said.

"We should check out the caldera!" Raj exclaimed. "It's located at the top of the volcano. It's a series of about six circular holes. They look like dents or rings on the top."

I steered us towards the caldera of Olympus Mons. "Here we go!"

I let Raj and Yuna have a turn steering the MM, and then we gave Cozzie a turn. All of us had been super-careful and followed the line on the map as closely as we could. Not Cozzie! He steered the ship hard to the right and left and then up in a loop-the-loop! I felt as if I were on a roller coaster. I would have been worried that the ship might crash, but I knew that if he lost control, the ship's computers would take over.

"Now that is how you fly an MM," Mum said. Mum seemed to be having as much fun as we were.

We let Cozzie steer the ship until we reached the outer edge of Olympus Mons. When we did, I took the controls

again. The outer edge of Olympus Mons was high, so I pulled back on the controls, sending us up the side.

The MM gave another boost and our speed picked up a lot. I held on tight to the controls.

When we were almost four miles up, we had reached the top of the cliff and the surface leveled off. It went from being steep like a cliff to more flat like a hill.

"Are we on the top?" Cozzie asked.

"Not even close," Mum said. "We're only at the top of what's called a scarp. The rest of Olympus Mons rises very slowly from here to the caldera. It won't even feel like we're climbing a volcano because it's so gradual."

I accelerated and the Martian Master zoomed high above the surface. The landscape below seemed to go on forever in every direction. We'd travelled a long distance when we finally flew over an edge that dropped way off.

"The caldera!" Yuna exclaimed. It was a gigantic hole. Red dust swirled below, making it hard to see all the way to the bottom.

"Let's land and check it out," Mum suggested.

Raj pressed the button on the screen, and before we knew it we were on the surface, parked near the edge of the caldera.

We got out and took pictures of ourselves near the edge. Mum made sure we stayed back far enough so no one fell off. I sent a picture to Tia and Allison. Raj and Yuna were also on their phones, sending pictures to their friends back on Earth.

My phone buzzed. It was Tia and Allison texting back.

Allison wrote: *Where are you?*

Tia texted: *They're on top of Olympus Mons! That is the coolest picture I've ever seen!*

I wrote: *We're going down into the caldera. I'll send more pictures in a little while.*

I looked towards the edge of the caldera and felt a surge of anxiety. It reminded me of just how dangerous it was on Mars. We were the only humans around for miles. If something went wrong, we were on our own.

"Who wants to go to the bottom?" Mum asked.

I felt uneasy about going to the bottom. Mum said we were safe, but I sure didn't feel that way. *Maybe they were on to something when they named the moons Deimos and Phobos*, I thought.

"Is it safe?" I asked Mum.

Cozzie's eyes bulged. "If Starr is afraid, there's no way I'm going down there."

"I'm not afraid," I said. "I'm just a little nervous."

"I wouldn't go in if I didn't think it was safe," Mum added.

I nodded and we all climbed back in the MM. Mum took over the controls, just to be extra safe. She rolled the MM to the edge and then accelerated off. The MM switched from rolling to hovering automatically. She began the descent down into the caldera. The Sun had been behind us, and as soon as we dropped down a bit, we were in shadow. I could tell from looking at the map on the screen that the caldera is a series of circular shapes. The thought of going to the bottom was terrifying and amazing.

"Imagine what this was like millions of years ago," Raj said. "There might have been lava flowing all over the place."

"I'm glad it's not anymore!" Cozzie said.

When we finally reached the bottom, we climbed out. I knew that we were in a gigantic, circular-shaped hole, but the hole reached so far across to the other side that we couldn't even see where it ended. There was also a lot of dust floating around, which made it harder to see. I felt so tiny.

We took lots of samples and loaded them back in the MM. I tried as hard as I could to calm down, but I couldn't. There was something about being in the caldera that made me feel really nervous.

It didn't seem to bother Raj, Yuna, or Mum. Yuna found a spot tucked away behind several large boulders that seemed like a tiny cave protected from the wind. She took a tube of paint and a brush from her backpack and quickly painted a picture of all of us on the side of one of the rocks.

"Martian cave art," she said proudly.

I took a few pictures of it as a record of the very first Martian drawings by a human. Mum loved it!

We loaded the last of the rock samples in the Martian Master and climbed back in to head back to the station. We had been there a few hours, and Mum said we should get back to the others. I was ready to get back to the safety of the station.

Mum pressed the button to turn the MM back on — and nothing happened.

Chapter 8

GLITCH

We all fell super-silent as she tried it again: still nothing.

"What's wrong?" Cozzie asked, panic and fear definitely in his voice. "Why won't it start?"

Mum kept trying, but she couldn't get the MM to start back up. My heart thumped so hard in my chest I could feel it beating.

"I bet it's the dust," Raj said. "It was blowing all over while we explored the caldera."

I felt my jaw clench and noticed Yuna nervously

tapping her foot. "What happens if we can't get it started?" Yuna asked.

"We'll get it started," Raj said. "Let's call the professor and ask him for a little help?"

Mum pressed the button to make the call, but it didn't work. I tried making a call with my phone and that didn't work either. None of the phones worked. We were stranded.

"I think that we're so deep in the caldera that the phone signals aren't working," Mum said. "I don't know why the MM isn't working, though. It should be fully functional and able to operate in these conditions."

I remembered the soccer ball hitting the bottom of the MM earlier and felt a ping of hope. "Maybe it has something to do with the soccer ball hitting the bottom," I suggested.

"I bet that had something to do with it!" Raj exclaimed. "I'll go take a look."

He climbed back out of the MM and vanished

underneath. We all climbed out too. I knelt down to see what he was up to, and he already had a piece of the bottom panel off. "It looks like the ball might have knocked it loose," he said. "There's a bunch of dust on the wiring. I bet it's the problem. I'm not sure how I'm going to get the dust off."

We looked inside the MM for anything that might help get off the dust, but couldn't find anything. "I have a few more paintbrushes in my backpack," Yuna said. "Maybe we can use them to dust off the wiring."

"That might work," Raj said. She handed them to him, and he worked for a while dusting off the wires. The Sun had set, and the caldera felt even creepier. Above I spotted Deimos and Phobos in the sky. Cozzie noticed them too.

"This place is cursed," he said.

"It's not cursed," Mum insisted. "We're just having a technical glitch. I bet we get the MM working again in no time at all."

"Give it a try," Raj said.

"Cozzie, why don't you click the starter this time?" Mum asked. "You might give us a little luck."

Cozzie climbed in, crossed his fingers, and pressed the starter. The MM started right up as it had earlier in the day. We all cheered. Raj quickly put back the panel and climbed out from under it.

"Those brushes did the trick," Raj said. "You should bring your art supplies with you wherever you go."

"I always do," Yuna said.

We made it back from Olympus Mons long after the other Martian Masters arrived. By the time we returned, everyone else was already back inside the station, except for Dad. He was recording as we approached.

We landed softly on the surface, near the other MMs. Dad stopped recording and hugged us all after we climbed out. Raj's and Yuna's families were inside the station waving like crazy from one of the pods. They both skipped towards the station.

"Thank goodness you are all right," Dad said. "We were really worried about you."

"We're fine," Mum said. "We just had a little glitch."

"It was pretty scary," Cozzie said. "But it was also pretty exciting."

"If you thought that was exciting, wait until tomorrow when we visit Valles Marineris!" Mum said.

CAMPING TRIP

The next morning, I was in Mum's office. She sat at her desk, looking at three different computer screens. Two of them had maps displayed, and the third had a live chat with Mrs Sosa. "Hi, Starr," Mrs Sosa said.

"Hi, Mrs Sosa," I replied.

"I watched the video from Olympus Mons yesterday. Simply remarkable," she said. "You are all doing a wonderful job. People on Earth are very excited about what's going on up there."

"It was definitely exciting," I said.

"How are Raj and Yuna doing?" Mrs Sosa asked.

"Good." I replied. "It was hard at first because we couldn't communicate very well. But we created new audio translation software for our helmets, and it's made a huge difference."

"That's great!" Mrs Sosa replied.

"Mum, can I go out to the greenhouse pods and help Kathy?" I asked.

"Have breakfast first and then you can go help her."

I raced to breakfast and then to Professor Will to suit up and head out to help Kathy. He came out with me. Kathy's greenhouse pod wasn't far from the station.

"How's it going in here?" Professor Will asked when we'd gone inside.

"So far, so good," she said. "I've mixed the Earth soil with various Martian soils. It's going to be interesting to see in which ones the crops grow best. I can create near-perfect conditions for growing here. There are no pests such as insects or small animals to destroy the crops."

I helped Kathy move crops into the new planting beds for almost two hours.

"We should head back to the station, Starr," the professor said. "The group is leaving for Valles Marineris soon."

"I'm going to stay here and continue on the farm," Kathy said. "There's so much work to be done. I can't wait to hear all about your trip, though."

I had been so focused on farming that I hadn't noticed that Professor Will had been going back and forth to line up all the Martian Masters outside. One of the Martian Masters had several pods attached to it.

We said goodbye to Kathy, I put on my suit, and we went out onto the surface.

"We've decided to stay over at Valles Marineris for a few days," the professor said. "We'll tow a few pods behind us so we don't have to keep making the trip back and forth to the station for somewhere to sleep. It means we can spend more time there too."

"I didn't even realize we could move pods around like that!" I said, astonished.

"I have a lot of tricks up my sleeve," the professor said with a wink.

Inside the station, everyone was doing their last-minute packing to prepare for the trip to Valles Marineris.

Mum was still at her desk when I walked in. "Hey, Farmer Jane," she said, smirking.

"Hey," I said. "I didn't realize we were going to Valles Marineris for a few days."

"Sure! We'll leave most of the pods here so we can have the main station near Olympus Mons, and we'll set up a new, smaller station over by Valles Marineris."

"What about Raj and Yuna?" I asked.

"We're all coming along! It's going to be quite an adventure. Why don't you go grab anything you want to take with you and meet me back here in a little while?"

About an hour later, we were all packed up and

loaded into the MMs. I sat in the back with Cozzie and Apollo, while Mum and Dad sat in the front. We took off and followed the other MMs and Professor Will. His MM pulled several pods behind it.

"I can't believe how powerful the MMs are," Mum said. "I would have never imagined that it would be strong enough to pull a line of pods."

The MM looked like a train, and the pods were like the train cars pulling behind it. "All aboard!" Cozzie announced, pulling his arm as if he were pulling a train whistle.

Chapter 10

BIG TROUBLE

We made it to Valles Marineris safely after a long journey. Professor Will landed the pods in a long string along the surface as the Sun set. Each family had its own pod. It was like we were on a camping trip on Mars.

We were so tired from the trip that we went to bed early. I slept like a Martian rock that night. I dreamed about flying around Mars in the MM.

In the morning, Raj, Yuna, and I were outside playing soccer when the professor approached us.

"I have a fun experiment that I thought you and your

team might want to help me with today," Professor Will said.

"What is it?" I asked.

"I'd like to tow several pods out to different locations within Valles Marineris. Each one contains a different experiment."

"How can we help?" Raj asked.

"You guys can tow them out with an MM."

"It sounds like fun to me," Yuna said.

"I already asked your parents if it's okay for you to help. It should be easy enough," the professor said. "I'll be able to track you on my computer."

He showed us how to connect a pod to the back of the MM. It was pretty amazing because the tube from the pod connected to the MM, so you could actually move between the MM and the pod.

We flew the first two out to the locations without any trouble, but when we were about halfway to the location with the third, the sky started to fill with red dust like

I've never seen before. *Maybe Cozzie is right and Mars is cursed*, I thought. The surface below vanished completely as we were swallowed up in the dust storm.

"Press 'Land,'" Raj said. I pressed the landing feature, but nothing happened. Then the map vanished from the screen and the dashboard lights blinked off.

"What's happening?" Yuna asked, alarmed.

"The dust must be short-circuiting the system," Raj said. "Try to lower it the best you can."

I did my best to lower the MM slowly, even though I couldn't see where I was going. I figured that if I went slowly, when we finally reached the ground we hopefully wouldn't hit very hard. We had been travelling pretty high, and it took a few minutes before we finally touched down on the surface with a thud. The impact wasn't too bad, but almost immediately the MM started moving.

"We must have landed on a steep incline," Yuna said. "We're sliding."

I tried to lift back up, but it didn't work. The MM

tipped on its side, and we bounced and tumbled down what must have been a steep cliff. When we finally reached the bottom, I was amazed we weren't hurt. My neck hurt a little from the impact, but other than that, I felt fine. "Wow, we were lucky," I said.

Raj and Yuna spoke at the same time, and I realized I couldn't understand anything they were saying. I banged the side of my helmet with my hand to jar the wires. It was no use; the translator wasn't working. We were back to three different languages. We were in big trouble, and we all knew it.

I didn't have to understand what they were saying to know how they were feeling. All I had to do was look into their eyes. They were panicked and worried. I felt the exact same way. Raj was talking super-fast, and I knew that he must have been saying something about our situation and how we were going to get out alive.

I located my phone and tried to make a call to the station, but it didn't go through. Panic rushed through me as I watched Raj and Yuna do the same. None of the phones worked.

After a few panic-filled minutes, I realized I had to calm myself somehow. I was the leader, after all. Raj and Yuna were my responsibility. I had been trained for this sort of thing. I took a few deep breaths to calm my mind and tried to focus. Mum had taught me that in an emergency you have to focus on all the positives.

Focus on the positives, I thought. *We're alive — that's a big positive. We have oxygen. The space suits are still doing their jobs.* The suits were providing us with oxygen and were keeping us warm too. So we had oxygen and warmth. It was important to focus on those things.

The negatives, I thought. Mum had always taught me that the negatives should not be ignored in an emergency, but you have to focus on the positives before you can deal with the negatives. First of all, we were lost. That was a big negative. Also, we had no way to communicate with the station. If that wasn't enough, we didn't know if everyone else was safe. I was sure there were more negatives, but I couldn't think about them without getting upset again.

Raj and Yuna were still trying to communicate with me, but I had no clue what they were saying. We finally sat and all fell silent. We were lost on Mars.

Chapter 11

LIGHTBULB

Raj took his phone apart, trying to figure out a way to make it work. He held out his hands and indicated that Yuna and I should give him our phones. He took them apart too. None of them worked.

Yuna pointed to the phones and shook her head from side to side. It was clear she thought that Raj should shut down the phones to save the charge. She was right. We couldn't afford to have the phone batteries run out of charge. The lights might be the only things we had that could save us.

After a few hours of pointing and miming at one another, the sense of seriousness grew even greater. The dust storm had been making the sky pretty dark earlier, but after the sunset, we were now in complete darkness. Thankfully, somehow our suits were still keeping us warm.

It was the longest night of my life. Morning came, and the Martian surface was slightly visible. The storm wasn't completely over, but it was clearing. Our phones didn't work, and the MM was dead. We had to get a plan together. The expedition might not come looking for us until the conditions were safer, and we had no food or water.

I searched frantically through my pockets, which I had done countless times already. I had nothing but rock samples I'd collected. Raj had a few small tools and some wires. Yuna reached in her pockets and pulled out a hair clip, some candies, and two tubes of green paint. I wished I'd brought something that might help save us.

Yuna pretended to squeeze the paint into her mouth and eat it. We all smiled and giggled a little. It was the first time something seemed funny since the storm.

Suddenly, an idea hit me like a Martian hurricane. The green paint! I remembered that Cozzie had told me green would stand out against the red surface. The MM was green, but it was covered with dust from the storm. For some reason, the dust didn't seem to stick to the pod as much. There were still plenty of places where we could see out.

I motioned to Yuna that I needed to use the paint. I took it, squeezing some of the paint out of the tube and onto my hand. Then I spread it on a part of the pod that wasn't covered by red dust. Raj and Yuna realized what I was doing and joined in. We smeared the green paint all over the spots of the pod that were still clear. I thought about going out of the pod to wipe off some of the dust, but didn't want to risk something going wrong and putting us in even more danger.

Raj took out our phones and tried calling one more time. They still didn't work. He powered them off to save the batteries. We waited all day, but no help came. The day seemed to drag on forever.

When darkness fell again, Raj clicked the phones back on and programmed them to blink on and off rapidly. Then he placed one up to a spot we'd smeared with green paint. He handed each of us a blinking phone and pointed to a green spot on the surface of the pod. It was a great idea. The blinking phones would light up the green portions of the pod, making it look like a giant green lightbulb. From the outside, it should be visible to anyone looking for us.

We were excited for a while and had a new sense of hope. It slowly wore off as each passing minute went by. After about an hour, my arm had grown completely numb from holding up the phone.

I wasn't sleeping, but I wasn't fully awake either. That's when I heard voices outside the pod. The green

paint blurred everything, but I could make out figures moving around outside. "Starr!" I heard Mum shout.

"In here! We're in here!" I called.

"Are you okay?" she asked.

"Kind of."

"Do you have your suits on?" she asked.

"Yeah," I shouted.

"Stand back," Professor Will warned as he cut a hole in the side of the pod with a saw.

We were saved. I had never been so thankful in all my life.

Mum hugged me tight and pulled in Raj and Yuna. "Thank goodness you're okay. We've been searching everywhere for you."

"Our phones didn't have any signal," I said. I was shaking and talking a mile a minute.

"It was a brilliant idea to paint the inside of the pod green and use your phones to create light," Professor Will said. "We spotted you the moment we flew over the edge of this canyon. It's a good thing you guys were able to communicate and work together."

I smiled. "That's the amazing thing," I said. "None of our technology was working properly, but we still found a way to work together."

When we returned to the station, everyone was thrilled that we were all right. It had been a really frightening experience, but we had survived.

We spent a few more weeks on Mars before returning home to Earth again. The mission had been a success. Mum was happy because we had collected lots of samples to take back to Earth, and she'd somehow managed to keep everyone safe.

Dad was thrilled too. He said he had enough film to make an amazing documentary about our trip to Mars.

Kathy and the professor had set up the first greenhouses on Mars. If we returned in the future, there would be plenty of food growing and ready to eat.

On the day we left, we passed by Deimos and Phobos

for the last time. I thought about all of the panic and fear I had felt on Mars and wondered if these names did mean something after all. Was the planet cursed? I figured I'd never really know. After all, I had survived, and the experience had been totally out of this world!

ABOUT THE AUTHOR

Raymond Bean is the best-selling author of the *Benji Franklin*, *Sweet Farts*, and *School Is a Nightmare* books. He teaches by day and writes by night. He lives in New York with his wife, two children, and a Cockapoo named Lily. His bags are packed for the day when space-cations become a reality.

ABOUT THE ILLUSTRATOR

Matthew Vimislik is an illustrator and game designer working in Rochester, NY. He lives with his wife, two cats, and possibly a family of Black-billed Cuckoo birds that has made a nest in his meticulously preened hair.

OUT of THIS WORLD

I'm Starr and I'm just like every other ten-year-old girl I know, with one big difference ... I live in space!

You see, my mum is a world-class astronaut, scientist and all round super genius. Now she's not just my mum, she's also in charge of the world's most advanced space station. People can visit here on holiday and it's my job to make sure they have a great time. My best friend, Allison, thinks I'll forget all about her now that I live in space, but just because I live in space doesn't mean I don't need my best friend. I may be a regular girl, but my life is completely out of this world!

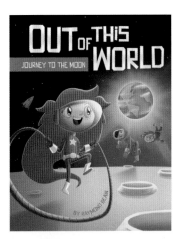
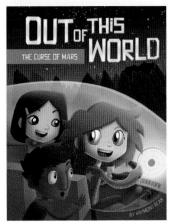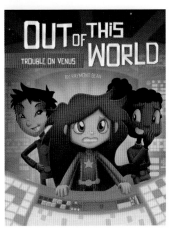

READ THEM ALL!

ROLL UP, ROLL UP!

Meet Lizzie Brown, the circus's youngest ever fortuneteller, and her friends, the crime-solving Penny Gaff Gang!

Lizzie Brown has escaped the slums of Victorian London and joined Fitzy's Travelling Circus. By accident, she discovers that she has an amazing ability: in a world of charlatans and tricksters, Lizzie may be the only truly clairvoyant palm reader in existence! Lizzie musters together her gang of circus children – the Penny Gaff Gang, all with their own amazing talents – to use her visions to solve mysteries.

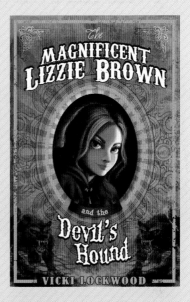

For more exciting books from
brilliant authors, follow the fox!

www.curious-fox.com